DUELING DIARIES

Ivy Hall School
1072 Ivy Hall Lane
Buffalo Grove, IL 60089

Based on the TV series *Angela Anaconda*®
created by Joanna Ferrone and Sue Rose as seen on the Fox Family Channel®

SIMON SPOTLIGHT
An imprint of Simon & Schuster Children's Publishing Division
1230 Avenue of the Americas, New York, New York 10020

© 2001 DECODE Entertainment Inc.
Copyright in Angela Anaconda and all related characters is owned by DECODE
Entertainment Inc. ANGELA ANACONDA is a registered trademark of Honest Art, Inc.
FOX FAMILY and the FAMILY CHANNEL names and logos are the respective trademarks of
Fox and International Family Entertainment.
All rights reserved.

SIMON SPOTLIGHT and colophon are registered trademarks
of Simon & Schuster.

Manufactured in the United States of America

First Edition

2 4 6 8 10 9 7 5 3 1

ISBN 0-689-83993-6

(family)

Angela Anaconda™

DUELING DIARIES

by Kent Redeker

Simon Spotlight

New York   London   Toronto   Sydney   Singapore

Dear Diary,

Hello Diary. My name is Angela Anaconda, and I will name you, **"Angela's Secret, Private Diary."** So now we both have names. My dad, who is **cool**,  gave you to me, and I am going to write all about me in you so that you will understand that I am way <u>better</u> and <u>way more interesting</u> than Nanette Manoir.

Dad

Dearest Diary,

I have decided to keep a journal, or diary if you will. Why? you may ask. Well I have been thinking that since there's only one of

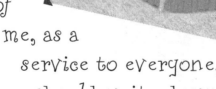

me, as a service to everyone, I should write down my memoirs, so that someday, everyone might have insights on how to be a more me-like person.

Dear Diary,

Our class took a field trip to the Space Museum today. I wore my cool **bright orange** space jumpsuit—just like Astronaut Bob the astronaut wears! But **Ninny Head Manoir** had to go and wear a silver space cadet outfit with a matching space hat that looked like it was a giant tinfoil **SPIFFY-POP**. And when she made fun of my dad's special moon rock I brought, I thought about stuffing her in a giant **MICROWAVE**.

Astronaut Bob

Dearest Diary,

Today was our class trip to the space museum. I wore my très appropriate space-inspired designer outfit. Unfortunately, my attempts to make our class seem classy were ruined by Angela Anaconda and her orange monkey suit. She also brought a rock that was supposedly from the moon. I couldn't help suggesting, dear diary, that maybe it was one of the rocks from her head.

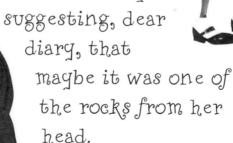

Dear Diary,

Today I invented my **new** favorite lunch for lunch that I have decided is my **FAVORITE**! It is **baloney and ketchup sandwiches**, and they are the best! Except I put so much

ketchup on them that some dripped

on my shoe, but who cares because the sandwiches were **so good!**

Here I am doing my **"New Favorite Lunch"** Dance

Dearest Diary,

Today, lunch was a complete disaster! Cook forgot to remove the crusts on mon petit cucumber sandwiches. I realize that I already have brains and beauty, but would it be too much to ask that my lunch not be ruined by blatant carelessness? I'll have to speak to Mummsy about lowering his Christmas bonus next year.

Dear Diary,

Today I helped my dad with one of his **inventions**, which isn't really an invention because it hasn't been all the way invented yet. He says he saw an alarm clock on this TV commercial that was powered by a **POTATO**. I don't know how, but Dad says it is true. So, he is trying to invent a **can opener** that will be powered by a **cucumber**! I hope it works on account of the fact that everyone will buy up all the cucumbers to open cans with, and no one will try to cut them up and put them in **jiggly fruit** anymore!

Dad

Dearest Diary,

Today Mummsy showed me how to make frozen cucumber rounds for puffy eyes. Then, we lay out in the sun with them over our eyes. Mummsy says beauty is a skill that even one so naturally beautiful as moi cannot take lightly!

Mummsy

Dear Diary,

I have decided **noT** to take King to obedience school anymore on account of—okay, maybe she cannot sit or roll over, but who

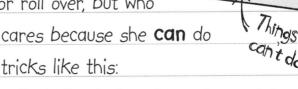

Things I can't do

cares because she **can** do tricks like this:

* Finding lost socks and a certain somebody's French poodle

* Going to the **bAthroOm** on the Nanette statue that is **SO UGLY** that even her own mom didn't want it

* Opening doorknobs with her mouth

* Finding one tiny bit of leftover **ChinEse fooD** in a whole bagful of **TRASH**

PLEASE RELEASH ME
OBEDIENCE SCHOOL

King

Dearest Diary,

I have decided that I won't be taking Oo-la-la to obedience class any longer. The other dogs there are simply a bad influence on him. Besides, here are the tricks that I've already trained Oo-la-la to do at a competitive show-dog level.

* Shake hands with royalty
* Blow "kisses"
* Sniff luggage for explosives
* Speak—in English and French
* Curtsy
* Tell true designer fragrances from cheap imitations

Oo-la-la

Dear Diary,

I know you probably won't believe me, but I actually had a **goOd day** at school today. And

that is on account of Mrs. Brinks was out **sick**! We had a substitute teacher named Geri Klump who actually was a teacher who actually **LiKED** me on account of she had so many **freckles** like me.

She even sat with me and Johnny and Gina at lunch! Maybe Mrs. Brinks will **never** get better, or decide to **RETiRe** or something and then Geri will be here **all the time!**

Good-bye, Mrs. Brin
Have a nice retiremer

P.S. That's what she let's us call her. . .Geri!

Dearest Diary,

Today was unbearable! Mrs. Brinks was taken *ill* and they replaced her with some horrid substitute named Klump. (What kind of name is that?) I don't see how the school board can allow such incompetent individuals in the classroom. I hope Mrs. Brinks gets well, and soon! Maybe Mummsy and Daddy are right, maybe we should consider Swiss boarding school after all.

Dear Diary,

Tomorrow is the annual Teamathon Race, and Gina Lash, who is on my team—the Team Lemon—is still not in running shape. I have assigned Gordy Rhinehart to be her personal trainer. Here are two things he has tried:

GORDY

1. Making her drink nutritious vegetable shakes

2. Making her run away from him by threatening to KISS her (This one really did the trick!)

Gina

16

Dearest Diary,

Tomorrow is the annual Teamathon Race and I *still* don't have anything to wear! It is so hard to find fashionable sportswear to match the green pinnies of our team—the Team Lime! Even Le Sportique was no help! Often I think I'm just far too fashionable for Tapwater Springs. Woe is me!

Dear Diary,

Josephine Praline says that I should try to be **NICER** to Ninnie Wart. So I am trying to think of things that are nice about Nanette to put in a list.

MY LIST OF GOOD THINGS ABOUT NINNIE WART:

1. She's not a twin.

2. She doesn't have a clone.

3. There's only one of her.

Josephine

"Hey, Ninnie, do you want half of my ANT sandwich?"

Dearest Diary,

It occurred to me that not everyone may know all the good things about me. Like for instance...

MY LIST OF GOOD THINGS ABOUT MYSELF:

1. My sparkling blue eyes
2. My exquisite eyelashes
3. My perfect golden curls
4. The way I wear my beret just right
5. My lush alto-soprano voice
6. The flawless way I perform my arabesque
7. The dimples on the backs of my knees
8. My petite ankles
9. My ability to properly place a napkin across my lap...

Sorry, Ninnie Poo. I hate to interrupt, but I realize that this list could go on for, like, seventeen more pages, but the editors of this book are worried that we will not have enough paper to print it all!

Dear Diary,

Today at show-and-tell I have something **great** to show that everyone is going to think is great! What I am talking about is my genuine private-eye pen for private eyes! It can write upside down, in the DaRK, and also **underwater**. It even has a tiny tape recorder for recording **secret** private eye stuff. I know this will be good because no one has **ever** brought a show-and-tell like this to school before! Even Nanette Manoir can't top this!

ANGELA

GOOD SPY GEAR

Dearest Diary,

Today, I have decided to bless the class with a special show-and-tell extravaganza. I am bringing in private eye Dirk McGirk, who is on permanent retainer with my family. He is going to tell how he solved "The Mystery of the Laughing Globe" and other très interesting stories. I'm sure the class will once again be grateful to me for enriching their otherwise dreary lives. It's not my problem that it happens to be Angela Anaconda's turn. She never has anything good to show anyway.

Ha ha ha ha!

Dear Diary,

Mapperson's Bakery is having a contest to find a **NEW faCe** to be on the side of their truck and I have to **WIN** so that **Ninnie Wart's** face is not driving around Tapwater Springs on the side of a truck! Here is my list of things to do that will help me win:

* Wash my face before I go to Mapperson's
* Wash Mr. Mapperson's window with Dad's new invention— the **SqueeGee-EaSy**
* Eat more muffins than Nanette (maybe Gina Lash can help me)

Dearest Diary,

Here is my checklist of things I will do to ensure the people of Tapwater Springs will have the pleasure of seeing my beautiful face on the side of Mapperson's gross truck:

* Have Johnny Abatti carry a sandwich board, with my face on it, around the block
* Put my face on helium balloons
* Pretend to eat lots of Mapperson's muffins, but actually feed them to Oo-la-la when no one is looking

Nanette

Manoir

Dear Diary,

    I found out that I didn't win the Mapperson's face contest. But that is okay on account of NincoMPOOPULa didn't win either! In fact, the winner was my best friend, **Gina Lash**! And she  won fair and square because Mr. Mapperson said she was his **BEST** customer. I was happy because Nanette didn't win, and Gina was happy because she got **all-you-can-eat cinnamon swirls** for the rest of the day!

I love cinnamon swirls!!

Dearest Diary,

It's not fair! That friend
of Angela's, Gina Lash, actually
beat me! Angela and Gina must
have gotten together and bribed
Mr. Mapperson! Well, I told Daddy
to sell all our stock in Mapperson's
Bakery immediately, but he said
Mr. Mapperson owns the whole
store and so there is no stock. Pooh!

Dear Diary,

This is most very unusual, I know, but tomorrow I cannot **wait** to go to **SCHOOL** on account of Dad got me a **brand-new** New England trench coat that is **NEW** and no one has ever had one before. So tomorrow I will have something that not even Ninkie Winkie will have a better one of and everyone will be **imPressed** with it (and **ME** who is wearing it).

Dearest Diary,

Tomorrow will be another day in the long list of days where Nanette Manoir sets the standard for style at Tapwater Elementary. That is because I will be sporting my brand-new English trench coat shipped directly from England (which is just kilometers away from France). It's an original, fashioned by the same tailor who makes chapeaux for Princess Anne.

I wonder if I shall ever tire of always being the first at everything?

Dear Diary

I can't believe it!!

Nanette Man-Copycat
copied my **GENUINE**,
new New England
trench coat!

SWEET
REVENGE!

Dearest Diary,

I guess I shouldn't have been surprised that Angela Anaconda tried to copy me. She's always been jealous of me. I'm just surprised that she found a coat that looked anything like mine. Not that someone with my fashion sense couldn't tell the difference a mile away.

Dear Diary,

Johnny Abatti is moving, and here is a list of things I need to get so I can throw a **better** going-away surprise party than Ninnie Poo:

* A real, live fireman
* Make that a real, live <u>singing</u> fireman
* Bobbing for apples with **MONEY** inside
* Racecar-shaped piñatas
* **Ten** Abatti's pizzas

JOHNNY

Dearest Diary,

Jonathan Abatti is moving and I am throwing him an elegant going-away soirée. Here's my soirée checklist:

* Hire a caterer
* Buy Mardi Gras costumes for January, Karlene, and moi
* Hire Pierre, Mummsy's party planner
* Hire French mimes (the pinnacle of artistic expression)
* Prepare a game of Epinglez la queue de l'âne (Pin the tail on the donkey)
* Pizza français

Karlene

January

Dear Diary,

It turns out Johnny isn't moving at all! He's just going to a **hotel** while his house is being **fumigated**. And best of all, Nanette got **SO MAD** when she found out he wasn't moving, that she left her going-away party—which was going on at Abatti's at the same time as ours!—and we got to have a **Nanette-less** party by ourselves!

YOU aRE NOW FRENCH FRIED!

Dearest Diary,

After all the effort I put into planning his going-away party, John has the nerve to tell me that he isn't moving at all. How thoughtless! Well as Mummsy says, you just can't trust men!

Dear Diary,

I don't have much time to talk today on account of I've decided that I have to break my <u>all-time</u> bubble-gum bubble blowing record! And to do so, I'll need **lots** of **PRACTICE**, so I brought home sixty-five cents worth of **gum** for me to practice with, so I'm going off to practice right **nOw**.

FIRST PLACE

Dearest Diary,

Well, it's off to baton-twirling practice for me. My baton recital is coming soon, and I feel I have a responsibility to the baton-twirling fans of Tapwater Springs.

...and step and spiiin...and look beautiful...and...

Dear Diary,

My backyard

Tonight I am writing by candlelight on account of Dad and I are **camping** in a **TENT** in the backyard. I get to sleep in *Trouty*, my fish-shaped sleeping bag. It has holes in it and smells like **pine trees** and **feet**, and Mom has tried to throw it out <u>three</u> times, but I won't let her on account of sleeping in a fish is the **best** thing about backyard camping!

P-U! ANGELA, THAT THING STINKS!

Mom

Dearest Diary,

Tonight, I'm writing by the light of our portable fireplace. I had Alfredo prepare the backyard camping gazebo, which is French for "fancy outdoor place." I ate sushi  and listened to the string quartet that we hired to come play. It was fun "roughing it" for one night, but

I'm anxious to get back to the pampering I deserve.

Dear Diary,

For you, Ninnie Poo!

Today was **volcano day** in class and everyone was supposed to make a volcano and Johnny and I made the volcano that was the **best one!** It was made out of **meatballs**, with Spaghetti-Sauce lava. But **NANETTE MAN-WARPED** showed up with a dinner plate that used to belong to some **FRENCH SCIENTIST** and called it a science project— and Mrs. Brinks actually **liked it** and gave Nanette an **A+** and gave everyone else a **C** without even looking at everyone's volcanoes. How can you get the **BEST VOLCANO GRADE** in class when you didn't even **make** a volcano? That's what I'd like to know!

Dearest Diary,

Today I enlightened the class by presenting a genuine place setting that was once used by famous French scientist Marie Curie. The actual assignment was somewhat less inspiring,

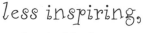

but it is my ability to "think outside the box" that sets me apart from the rest of my class.

Dear Diary,

Mrs. Brinks has just announced that **Valentine's Day** is coming up and everyone in class is supposed to make a valentine for everyone else in class and that includes **Ninnie Poo** who I now have to make a Valentine for. **YUCK!** Well, here it goes:

Here's the Valentine made for Gina

Roses are red.
Violets are **blue**,
If I were Nanette
I'd throw up on my Sl

"Save me, save me!" you will say.

Dearest Diary,

Although Mrs. Brinks requires us to make valentines for everyone in class, I wonder who in class truly deserves a card from Nanette Manoir? If only there was someone in class as beautiful as moi-self so that I might experience the same thrill all my classmates will feel upon receiving a valentine from me. Well, never mind. I may as well get Angela out of the way first:

Roses are red,
Violets are blue,
Angela Anaconda
belongs in a zoo.

Dear Diary,

I found one of Mrs. Brinks's "Stellar Student Star Stickers" on the floor next to her desk. She only ever gives them to **NANETTE**, so I have to put it here in you, Diary, where she'll never, **ever** see it.

Stellar Student

An apple a day doesn't keep Brinks away!!

♡♡♡

Dearest Diary,

If I don't stop earning Mrs. Brinks's "Stellar Student Star Stickers," I'm going to overfill my "star-board" at school. (I came up with the name

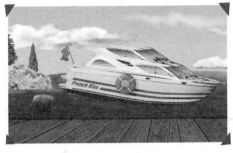

"star-board" because it reminds me of the right side of our yacht.) Anyway, I've decided to put some of the overflow stickers here until Mrs. Brinks makes me a new "star-board."

Stellar Student
Stellar Student
Stellar Student
Stellar Student
Stellar Student
Stellar Student
Stellar Student
Stellar Student
Stellar Student
Stellar Student
Stellar Student
Stellar Student
Stellar Student
Stellar Student
Stellar Student
Stellar Student
Stellar Student
Stellar Student
Stellar Student
Stellar Student
Stellar Student
Stellar Student
Stellar Student
Stellar Student
Stellar Student
Stellar Student
Stellar Student

Dear Diary,

Nonna

Today Johnny Abatti and I played in Nonna Abatti's **Aqua Pronto** lawn sprinkler. It was fun because you never knew where water would shoot up next and make you we**T**! I told Johnny he

JOHNNY

didn't have to wear scuba fins and scuba g**O**ggles, because it was only a **SPRINKLER**. But then he said that I didn't need to wear my inflatable **Sea-serpent floaty ring**. So then I quit teasing him on account of when I'm wet, I like to wear my floating sea-serpent floaty ring.

Dearest Diary,

Today was the day of the Manoir's annual *Bastille Day pool soirée*, which is French for "party only rich people can afford to throw." Some of my classmates (who I won't even mention) were *très gauche* enough to actually get into the *pool*. But not *moi*, of course. *Chlorine* would just ruin my perfect golden curls.

Dear Diary,

I am sorry to say that this is your **last page!** You have been a good friend to me and a **good listener** and that is why I am sorry that I left you in the **WASHING MACHINE**, and that King **buried you** in the garden, and also that it took me **two weeks** to find you and dig you up again. Maybe someday when I am older, I will come back and read you!

Until then, see you later when you see me!

Dearest Diary,

Well, Diary, you have come to an end. But do not despair. You are the *first* of many volumes in the tale of the *life* of Nanette Manoir. Ta-ta!

Ivy Hall School
1072 Ivy Hall Lane
Buffalo Grove, IL 60089